WALT DISNEY
PICTURES PRESENTS

THE
LION KING

SPECIAL EDITION

✴ *The* JOURNEY ✴

DVD COMPANION BOOK

Disney
EDITIONS
NEW YORK

With special thanks to the hundreds of animators, artists, and craftspeople at The Walt Disney Studios whose extraordinary work fill the pages of this book.

The book producer would also like to thank Don Hahn for his generous assistance.

Copyright © 2003 Disney Enterprises, Inc. Academy Award® is a registered trademark of the Academy of Motion Picture Arts and Sciences. IMAX® IMAX Corporation.

Photographs on page 66 from Disney's *The Lion King* stage production by Joan Marcus & Catherine Ashmore. Original London and Los Angeles Companies. In photographs: Fuscia, Paulette Ivory, and Roger Wright.

The following are registered trademarks of The Walt Disney Company: Walt Disney World Resort, Disney's Animal Kingdom, Kilimanjaro Safari.

For information address Disney Editions,
114 Fifth Avenue, New York, New York 10011-5690
www.disneyeditions.com

Produced by Welcome Enterprises, Inc.
6 West 18th Street, New York, New York 10011
www.welcomebooks.biz

Disney Editions Editorial Director: Wendy Lefkon
Disney Editions Editor: Jody Revenson
Project Director: Alice Wong
Designed by Timothy Shaner

Text by Jim Fanning
The Lion King Story text by Christopher Finch

Printed in U.S.A.

ISBN: 0-7868-5431-6

FIRST EDITION

1 3 5 7 9 10 8 6 4 2

Contents

The Journey Begins

The Journey Begins
by Don Hahn, Producer

Making an animated film, or any film for that matter, is a leap of faith. There's nothing to guarantee that the years of passion that get poured out onto the screen will amount to anything that an audience will want to see. When it does, it's fairly astounding. The history of *The Lion King* is fairly astounding.

The idea for an African story told with lions had been in development at the studio since 1989 in various forms and under various titles. After three years, hundreds of sketches, thousands of script pages, and a research trip to Africa, the clear story of Simba had still not emerged.

Then came a pivotal few days in early 1992 when directors

Rob Minkoff, Roger Allers, and I locked ourselves into an office in our warehouse studio with *Beauty and the Beast* directors Kirk Wise and Gary Trousdale, story supervisor Brenda Chapman-Lima, and a lot of paper and pizza. Two days later, a compelling story began to emerge: it was a love story between a father and his son—a love story that became stronger even as the lion cub grew.

As the story evolved, the next challenge came when the animators realized that they hadn't animated four-legged characters in years. It was time to go to school. We brought live lions into the studio. Animators traveled to the L.A. Zoo almost weekly to study the finer points of warthog locomotion, or meerkat anatomy. Through this homework we began to discover how this story could be told with a cast of characters that walked on four

legs and had no opposable thumb.

Animation is a medium that combines equal parts art, allegory, and alchemy. There is by nature nothing real about what we as filmmakers put on the screen. Yet somehow the ingredients of pencil, paper, pixels, and phosphor all combine in a craft that can put across very powerful emotions—emotions that feel very real to us even though they come from on-screen actors that are lions, meerkats, and warthogs.

Hard work and preparation can get you to a point, but then there are those days when fate steps in to indicate the direction. Score composer Hans Zimmer had done a stirring arrangement of the Elton John–Tim Rice anthem "The Circle of Life," but something was missing. We all knew that to establish the African setting, we wanted a more indigenous sound from the very

first frame of film. Hans asked us over to his studio one night. It was on that night, in that backroom studio, that vocal arranger and performer Lebo M experimented with ways to start the film. After a few takes, seemingly out of nowhere came the now famous cry in the wilderness that begins *The Lion King*.

No one could have imagined that this coming-of-age story about a lion cub who is blamed for his father's death would amount to much. In the early days of production, I had trouble getting people to work on the film. At times when *The Lion King* was at full throttle, we started to wonder what we had done, or if anyone would want to see it. I remember calling my sister and telling her I was working on a film— "sort of Moses and

Joseph meet Elton John and Hamlet in Africa." There was a very long pause on the other end of the line. Then she said: "Well, I hope it works out." It did.

From its inception under the title *King of the Jungle*, to long hours at the drawing board, to opening night at Radio City Music Hall, to the record-setting box-office success, to the Broadway musical inspired by the film, *The Lion King* has become, by anyone's definition, a phenomenon.

So when *The Lion King* was selected as the third in Disney's elite series of Platinum Edition DVDs, we found the prospect fairly astounding. The first two Platinum Edition DVD releases—*Snow White and the Seven Dwarfs* and *Beauty and the Beast*—are tough acts to follow. And since we knew firsthand the

Left above: 1994 original theatrical poster.
Left below: 2003 Special Edition DVD poster.

Lion King phenomenon, we wanted to create a DVD that would encompass all the many journeys that led to continents of creative adventure. It would, in short, need to be the king of DVDs.

Most of us were already DVD aficionados, and we jumped at the opportunity to create an entire DVD experience that would welcome you into all the realms of Simba's kingdom. The result is the greatest filmmaker participation of any Disney DVD yet produced. We're passionate about the film and we— artists, songwriters, animators— wouldn't have it any other way.

DVD means digital, of course, and that gave us a distinct advantage. *The Lion King* was one of the earliest films to be completed in a digital format using Disney's own Academy Award®–winning production system. This meant that back in 1994, each of the finished scenes in the film was stored as a digital file burned on CD (much like you would burn a CD on your home computer). In 2002, when it came time to prepare the film for its large-screen debut at IMAX® and large-format theaters, dozens of scenes were redrawn or digitally retouched to help the film play in this new giant format. For this DVD presentation— its first ever digital presentation—the film was completely enhanced and restored. And, in a DVD innovation fit for a king, we invited the Academy Award®-nominated Re-recording Mixer Terry Porter to create an all-new 5.1 Disney Enhanced Home Theater Mix—designed specifically for your home theater.

Best of all, from the perspective of the film's creators, we came full circle, if you will, and reunited for "Morning Report." Song composer Elton John and lyricist Tim Rice wrote this audience favorite for the

Broadway musical, so we decided
to produce all-new animation and
integrate it into the original film.
We think you'll enjoy revisiting
Simba, Mufasa, and Zazu as much
as we did.

In fact, revisiting *The Lion King*
for the Platinum Edition 2-Disc DVD
was an exhilarating experience
for the whole crew who worked
together to create it in the first place.
After careful digital restoration,
remastering, and recreating old
friends in new animation, and after
about a decade of unimaginable
events, we popped in that shiny
disc, turned on our TV, and did
what we had always hoped the
audience would do: we
were swept away by
the art, allegory, and
alchemy of animation
and the many wonders
of a very special love
story—*The Lion King*.

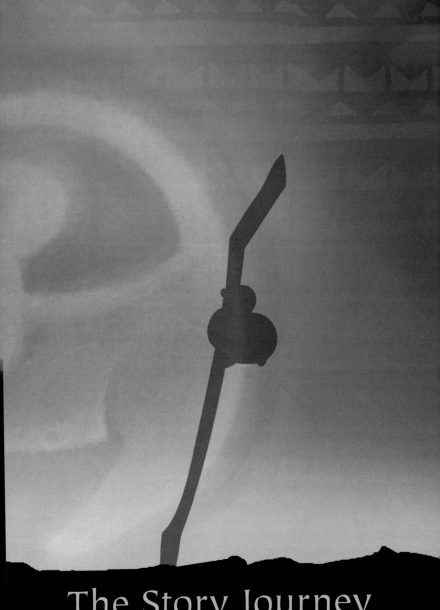

The Story Journey

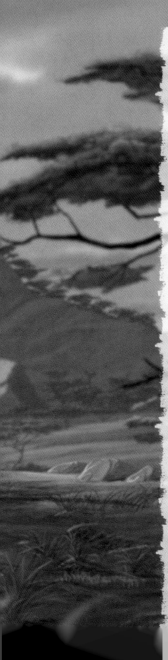

Inside the conference room, filled with story artists and animators, you can smell the felt-tip-pen ink, still wet on the latest story drawings. Enthusiastically, the film's directors begin to act out the story of their animated feature as sketched in hundreds of comic strip–like drawings. Engaged by the presenters' passion, you can see that for the artists who have crafted this story, this is more than another animated film—here, they have invested their hearts. Suddenly, you realize that the story you are experiencing is not a famous fairy tale or a literary classic—presented before you is an original story about animals on the African savanna. Surrounded by a panorama of storyboards, you sense something larger, deeper in this new story, something that touches your heart.

Left insets: Storyboard art.

As the screenwriters and story artists grappled with crafting an original story for *The Lion King*, their goal was to make their story emotionally authentic. As they imagined and reimagined the plot and action and characters, they realized that their developing story resonated with the power of a great myth. There was a connection with other primal stories that have endured for centuries, like the stories of Joseph and Moses from the Old Testament. It was Joseph who was born in royalty, then banished—only to return in a time of need, just as Simba fled and returned to Pride Rock. It was Moses who was spurred into action by the vision of a burning bush, just as Simba was strengthened by the vision of Mufasa. "We knew there was a kind of religious epic quality to *The Lion King*," remembers codirector Rob Minkoff.

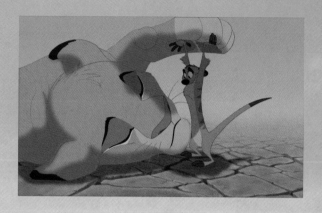

"The more you try to make [your film's story] authentic and true and deeper, and more resonant, the more it's going to be like the great myths that endure, that resonate now."
—JONATHAN ROBERTS, COSCREENWRITER

Another powerful story echoing throughout *The Lion King* is William Shakespeare's *Hamlet*. Would the once-and-future Lion King discover the inner strength to claim his rightful place as ruler? "From very early on, we were going to take on the telling of a story about coming of age," reveals codirector Roger Allers. One of the film's most compelling images is Simba's little paw going into Mufasa's paw print. "That had everything to do with ideas," observes producer Don Hahn, "and Rob and Roger had a strong idea about the dynamic between father and son, and the son taking his father's place, and that became very moving for the audience."

The *Hamlet* connection also challenged the filmmakers to reexamine the inner journey of Simba. "We all decided there needed to be a 'to be or not to be' scene, and it was the very last

"Remember who you are."

scene that was created for the movie," says Rob Minkoff. "After Mufasa visits Simba and leaves, Simba is left wondering what to do. This literally became our 'to be or not to be' moment. Everything after that became about being as good as that scene."

These compelling stories that emerged from within the material eventually led the creators to a discovery. "Finally we realized that the theme was responsibility. It's about leaving childhood and facing up to the realities of the world," recalls Don Hahn. "As the movie pulls together, the theme becomes more and more apparent in each scene," observes coscreenwriter Irene Mecchi. In the end, what evolved was a story far more powerful than anybody had anticipated. They had created *The Lion King*, a story of universal emotions that continues to resonate with audiences everywhere.

The Film Journey

The journey that began with a project called *King of the Jungle* and ended with an Academy Award®–winning masterpiece entitled *The Lion King* was a long one. The earliest script dates back to 1989 when the idea of making an animated feature about lions was first broached. As the film developed, producer Don Hahn had trouble attracting animators and artists to the project. "Let's face it, this lion cub gets framed for murder, we've got a wildebeest stampede, there's a singing warthog. Will it mean anything?" recalls Hahn. "It was the B picture," says story supervisor Brenda Chapman-Lima. "It was the one the A players weren't working on." But the artists who signed on for *The Lion King* began to see it as something special.

"The process of creation is a miracle. There is really no recipe and there's no path that is predetermined."

—PETER SCHNEIDER,
FORMER CHAIRMAN,
THE WALT DISNEY STUDIOS

In November 1991, a party from the studio traveled to Africa to discover the world of *The Lion King* for themselves. The team was astounded by the colors, vast vistas, and variety of wildlife they found. "The whole experience," says codirector Roger Allers, "helped bring everything into focus and allowed us to visualize the enchanted yet still realistic Africa that we wanted."

Soon after the expedition to Africa, the creative team knew it was time to determine the final outlines of the narrative. They sequestered themselves for two days, and a firm outline of the film emerged. "We made something that not one of us could have done on our own. And that is a very magical thing," reflects Don Hahn. The magic of *The Lion King* grew far beyond its creators' wildest expectations.

Right inset: Concept painting of gazelles.

"There was a day when our guide brought us to the top of a bluff, and it was as if you could see forever."

—CHRIS SANDERS, PRODUCTION DESIGNER

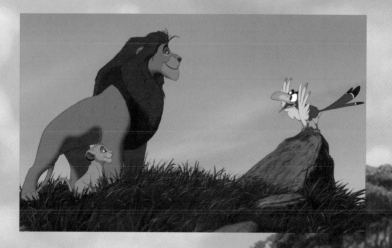

"Morning Report"

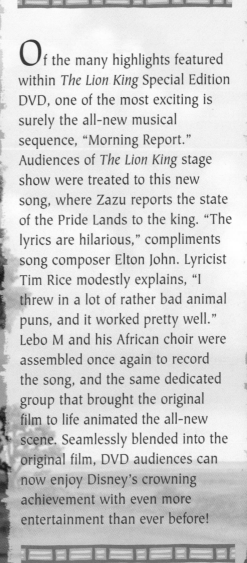

Of the many highlights featured within *The Lion King* Special Edition DVD, one of the most exciting is surely the all-new musical sequence, "Morning Report." Audiences of *The Lion King* stage show were treated to this new song, where Zazu reports the state of the Pride Lands to the king. "The lyrics are hilarious," compliments song composer Elton John. Lyricist Tim Rice modestly explains, "I threw in a lot of rather bad animal puns, and it worked pretty well." Lebo M and his African choir were assembled once again to record the song, and the same dedicated group that brought the original film to life animated the all-new scene. Seamlessly blended into the original film, DVD audiences can now enjoy Disney's crowning achievement with even more entertainment than ever before!

One frame at a time, *The Lion King* has been meticulously remastered and restored for its dazzling first ever digital presentation on DVD. "It's very gratifying to go now onto DVD with *The Lion King*," marvels codirector Roger Allers, "to see how much you can finesse the image, how much you can adjust the color to get it to accurately reflect all the intentions that you had originally. It's very satisfying."

Working from the film's original digital files, the original filmmaking team painstakingly and lovingly removed dust and dirt, added detail, and poured their hearts and talents into giving the home viewer a crisp, pristine restoration befitting the "king of all films!" Disney's top artists and technicians can take great pride in their accomplishment, which brings even greater clarity and vitality to this timeless classic.

Right insets: Before and after restoration.

A Restoration Befitting
the "King of All Films"

Who better than Zazu to guide you through the Pride Lands of *The Lion King* Special Edition DVD? With all-new 3-D animation created exclusively for the DVD menus and games, there is truly "more to see than has ever been seen." Supervised by the original *Lion King* team and produced by Walt Disney Feature Animation, the animals and environment of *The Lion King* have been recreated. Using original model sheets and animation backgrounds, your fabulous journeys into the varied realms of the DVD kingdom truly make this experience more than the movie. Now there really is more to see, more to hear and more to do than ever before in the "king of all DVDs!"

All-New Animation

The Animal Journey

In many ways, the story of Disney is the story of animals. Walt Disney often said that the Disney Studios were started by a mouse, and Mickey Mouse remains the world's most recognized and beloved animated star. Disney's first full-length animated feature, *Snow White and the Seven Dwarfs* (1937), costarred a forest full of lovable animals. For the landmark film *Bambi* (1942), Walt brought live animals into the studio not only for the artists to sketch and to create believable animal movements but also to study their personalities and behavior.

The Lion King continues this tradition. The film creators observed African animals on safari, in the zoo, and in special in-studio visits in order to create the beloved animated personalities of *The Lion King*.

"Sometimes we can recognize ourselves in animals—that's what makes them so interesting."
—WALT DISNEY

Here is a closer look at the true-life African animals that inspired the animated characters:

Lions usually live in prides, or groups, which consist of a male leader, adult females, and cubs. They are the only cats that live in large family groups. The male ruler, like Mufasa, marks and protects his territory with brute strength and a mighty roar that can be heard for five miles. The females, like Sarabi and Nala, are the hunters and are responsible for getting food for the pride. Because young males can be a threat to the ruler, they are often driven away. But like Simba returning to Pride Rock to fight Scar, the males sometimes come back when fully grown to challenge the existing leadership.

The happy duo of Timon and Pumbaa brings its humor and "no worries" attitude to Simba and the film. Their *hakuna matata* outlook is inspired by the live meerkats and warthogs the creative team observed. Real meerkats truly have a "problem-free philosophy": they spend most of their time sunbathing, grooming themselves, and sleeping. The meerkat is one of the few animals that can easily stand upright. This allowed the animators to use Timon's hands often in his slapstick humor. The Disney animators observed that warthogs bounce along with their tails straight up in the air, so they gave Pumbaa that same distinctive jolly walk. On the field trip to Africa, the animators were surprised to see grayish warthogs emerge bright red from rolling in the red dirt. Thus the animated Pumbaa is a happy red instead of a somber gray!

Hyenas and lions are true enemies in the wild. They compete for food, and their clashes are often violent and deadly. Hyenas are so ferocious they even attack one another. Like lions, hyenas live in groups, as many as 80 to a clan, and are fearsome predators. Hyenas hunt in packs, run up to 40 miles per hour, and can consume up to one third of their body weight in a feeding frenzy. Their powerful jaws can crunch up large bones, which is one reason the artists have the hyenas living in the Elephant's Graveyard. The distinctive appearance of Shenzi, Banzai, and Ed marks them as spotted hyenas. The spotted hyena has dark spots, reddish fur, and a sloping back, and is bigger than the striped hyena. Hyenas are most famous for their maniacal laughter-like howl. But as in *The Lion King*, the viciousness of the hyena is no laughing matter.

Animal-themed films such as *The Lion King* have always played an important role at The Walt Disney Company. Animals are also celebrated at Disney's Animal Kingdom®. This amazing Disney Theme Park at *Walt Disney World Resort®* ensures that visitors will be able to experience the unique Disney combination of animal facts and animal fantasy, for generations to come. At the center of Disney's Animal Kingdom is the Tree of Life, a 14-story wonder carved with images of more than 325 different animals. Its monumental style symbolizes the Circle of Life theme that defines *The Lion King*. It was the Kilimanjaro Safari® at Disney's Animal Kingdom that inspired an "experiential" feature in *The Lion King* Special Edition DVD: Timon and Pumbaa's Virtual Safari. Now Disney brings the strange and exciting animals of an African safari right to your living room.

"Animals have personalities
like people and must
be studied."
—WALT DISNEY

The Music Journey

As the red disk of the sun rises,
the one voice becomes many until
the Pride Lands echo with song.

The journey begins in silence. Filled with anticipation, you listen for the first note. Suddenly, the unfolding melody surrounds you, a song unfamiliar but resonating with emotion. Chills run up and down your spine as fingers dance up and down the piano keys, and a voice sings of new life, new possibilities. "There's far too much to take in here, more to find than can ever be found...." You feel the room resound with the new song, and the developing movie for which it has been composed takes on a new richness. Inspired by this flowing melody, the electricity of possibility unseen until now surges into the bright sun of creativity ... and it moves us all.

So much of the emotional vocabulary of *The Lion King* is music—and it's a language that eloquently speaks to us all in "The Circle of Life." It is difficult to imagine now, but at first, *The Lion King* wasn't envisioned as a musical. Lyricist Tim Rice was invited to consider the possibilities of transforming this fresh new story into a narrative told with lyric and melody. "'The Circle of Life' had to be—both lyrically and musically—a strong, powerful song that would also set some of the agenda for the film," says Rice. "I think perhaps my biggest contribution to the entire project was suggesting Elton John. I did say, well, you'll never get him because he'll be too busy. To my amazement, very quickly Elton came on board, and I was thrilled."

Above inset: Elton John, Tim Rice, (standing), Rob Minkoff, and Roger Allers.

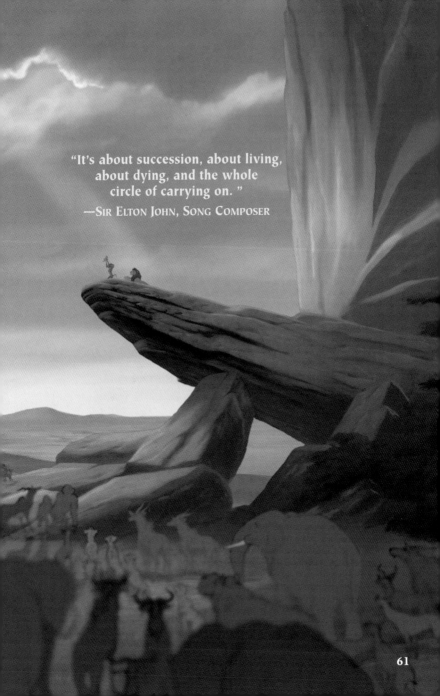

"It's about succession, about living, about dying, and the whole circle of carrying on."

—SIR ELTON JOHN, SONG COMPOSER

The music journey continued with the creation of the film's score, and score composer Hans Zimmer brought his own passion to the project. As with everyone involved with *The Lion King*, emotion was his keynote: "When you write a theme . . . you want to see how much life it really has, how many possibilities there are. Can it speak to you in joy, can it speak to you in sorrow? Can it be love? Can it be hate? Can you say all these things with just a few notes?" Zimmer asks. "The main emphasis was, for me, how are we going to get . . . to the idea that the father dies, and make it an emotional yet not horrifying experience, but make it something that children might actually want to start asking some questions about."

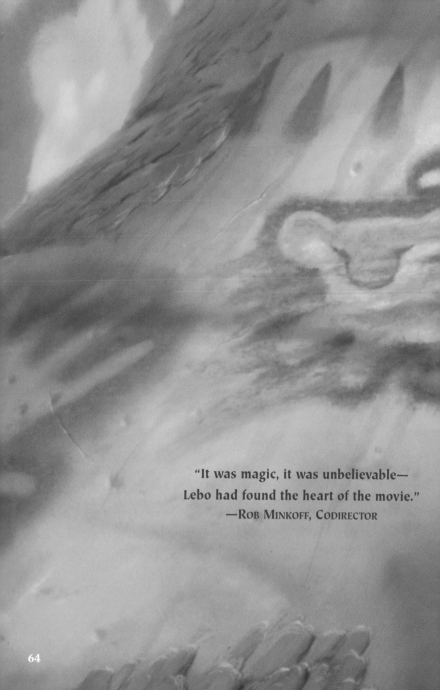

"It was magic, it was unbelievable—
Lebo had found the heart of the movie."
—ROB MINKOFF, CODIRECTOR

In Africa, Hans Zimmer had worked with a musician named Lebo M who the composer felt would bring authentic native lyricism to the songs and score. Incredibly, Lebo M wandered into the studio a few days before recording. Inspired by "The Circle of Life," Lebo M created an unforgettable native chant, a haunting cry that opens the film and immediately takes you to Africa. "It wasn't a bunch of Hollywood people trying to do what we thought it should be—it was some body from that place who was able to express his feelings about that place," explains Walt Disney Music president Chris Montan.

With the film's premiere, audiences embraced the songs of *The Lion King*—and the motion picture industry bestowed its highest honor. *The Lion King* won Best Original Song and Best Original Score at the Academy Awards®.

"The joy for me has been, and will always be, the process. The journey of *The Lion King* has gone further than any of us ever expected; where it will end only time and new audiences will tell."

—THOMAS SCHUMACHER, EXECUTIVE PRODUCER (FILM), PRODUCER (STAGE PRODUCTION) & PRESIDENT, DISNEY THEATRICAL PRODUCTIONS

"You see kids' faces, you see adults' faces when those animals walk through the theater at the beginning of the show and you're blown away. I get goose bumps thinking about it now."

—SIR ELTON JOHN, SONG COMPOSER

"Leaps of fantasy is something we try to do in our animated films, and something surely that Julie Taymor did on the stage."

—DON HAHN, PRODUCER OF ANIMATED FEATURE

The Stage Journey

The Lion King Story

In the velvet blackness
of an African night, at the
hour before dawn when
the land is full of dreams,
a lone voice heralds
the new day.

The red disk of the sun rises. The distant
mountain floats above the mist. Vast herds
move across the golden plain, and the Pride
Lands come alive with song.

High on Pride Rock, Mufasa the Lion King waits, watching as the creatures of his domain gather below to celebrate the arrival of the newborn prince.

Rafiki, keeper of the mysteries,
anoints Prince Simba's brow,
sprinkles the cub with ceremonial
dust, and raises him to the skies
for all of heaven and earth to see.

Mufasa's jealous sibling, Scar, sits in the shade, taking bitter pride in his absence from the sacred ceremony, scheming and dreaming of the day he will usurp the throne.

Zazu the hornbill, Pride Rock's chief of protocol, informs an indifferent Scar his truancy has not gone unnoticed. Confronted by Mufasa, Scar hides his rage beneath a cloak of scorn.

Each sunrise finds Simba in the royal cave, nudging his father from sleep, begging him to join in the ancient games that ensure the survival of the species.

From the peak of Pride Rock, father and son survey the Lion King's domain.

Crossing his kingdom, Mufasa speaks earnestly of the Circle of Life—the endless chain that links all living things, from the crawling ant to the leaping antelope.

Too young to read the fury in his uncle's eyes, Simba tells Scar all he has learned that day—how he, not Scar, will become the Lion King.

Sly Scar exacts a promise from the cub, a pledge that Simba will never venture near the forbidden place where the elephants go to die.

A graveyard!

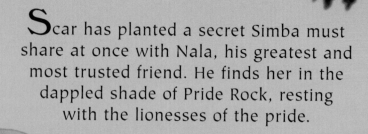

Scar has planted a secret Simba must share at once with Nala, his greatest and most trusted friend. He finds her in the dappled shade of Pride Rock, resting with the lionesses of the pride.

Simba and Nala can barely mask their curiosity, but first they must lose their escort, Zazu, sent along to keep mischief at bay.

Mistaking the cubs' whispered plans for love talk, Zazu imagines that romance is blooming. The cubs scoff at his quaint ideas and plot their escape.

Trying to elude their feathered guardian, the cubs play hide-and-seek.

Elephants and zebras, monkeys and giraffes join in the fun as Simba sings his song.

"I'm going to be

a mighty king!"

Escaping Zazu, the lion cubs arrive at the graveyard, an eerie spot littered with skeletons and monumental piles of bones.

From within a massive skull comes chilling laughter. A grinning trio of hyenas slinks into view: sinister Shenzi, scheming Banzai, and demented Ed.

Weaving among the skeletons, Simba and Nala flee, hyenas in pursuit. Zazu barely escapes with his feathers intact.

A roar seems to bring
the whole world to a stop.
The three hyenas freeze
until Mufasa's paw sends
them running.

Simba follows Mufasa home, planting his childish paws in his father's giant footsteps. Mufasa turns to face his son. Tears of regret glisten in Simba's eyes.

Mufasa talks of wisdom and folly, the difference between bravery and bravado, and explains how even a Lion King can know fear when he believes he may have lost a son he loves.

Night comes quickly to the Pride Lands. Mufasa and his son sit beneath the slowly turning galaxies. Mufasa passes along the wisdom of the pride, telling Simba how the great kings of the past look down from the stars and will always be there to guide him.

Meanwhile, Scar conceives a bolder
scheme, one that will rid the Pride Lands of
King Mufasa and the royal heir with one fell
swoop. Scar preens and poses on his rocky
pedestal, exhorting rank upon rank of
hyenas to greater heights of infamy.

With lies and wily flattery, Scar lures
Simba to a winding gorge and tells him
to wait there until Mufasa comes.

As Simba practices his roar, Scar signals
to his criminal confederates and sets
a tragedy in motion.

Simba hears a sound like thunder. Dust rises, and the earth begins to tremble. As he clings to a rotting tree, a tide of wildebeests sweeps by.

Scar warns Mufasa of Simba's peril,
sending his brother charging
into the path of the stampede.

With his last reserve of strength, Mufasa reaches up and places Simba on a ledge, safe from the panicked herd.

Scrambling to save himself, Mufasa sees his brother above him on the cliff, stretching out a helping paw.

Inch by inch, Scar pulls Mufasa toward safety but, at the last moment, lets him go and watches gleefully as Mufasa vanishes beneath the slashing hooves.

In the stillness that follows, Simba finds
a lifeless body sprawled in the dust.

As Simba sobs beside his father, Scar savors
his hour of victory. He plants seeds of
guilt and tells the bewildered cub
to flee far from the Pride Lands.

With Scar's hyena mercenaries in pursuit and gaining, Simba plunges from a bluff into the unknown.

The three hyenas watch as Simba vanishes, certain that the desert sun will finish off their work.

Eloquent with false grief, Scar reports the deaths of Simba and Mufasa to the pride.

When the usurper's hyena cronies lope into view, the lionesses recoil in horror.

On his perch Rafiki mourns
the loss of his friends.

Vultures circle overhead as Simba
collapses to the desert floor,
dazed by the blinding sun,
his legs too weak to carry on.

Eeeeeeeeeeeee—yaaaaaaaaaaaa!

With an earsplitting yell, Timon
the meerkat and Pumbaa the
warthog charge at the vultures.

As the ugly birds scatter, the two
friends see the lion cub near
death on the desert floor.

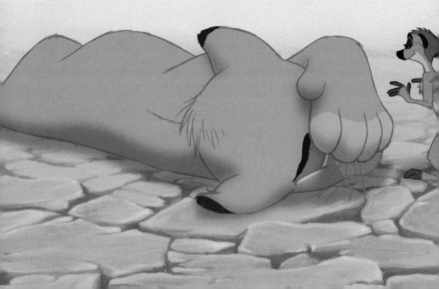

The cub seems so helpless; Pumbaa picks him up and carries him to the lush coolness of the nearby jungle.

When Simba awakes, Timon and Pumbaa persuade him to stay with them. They introduce him to their philosophy: *hakuna matata*—No worries!

Timon pulls back a fern, and Simba is introduced to his new friends' lair, a jungle paradise.

Succulent spiders, juicy beetles, and worms—Pumbaa and Timon initiate their new friend into the surprises of their creepy-crawly diet.

And so it happens that Simba, the lost crown prince, grows to manhood . . . far from the Pride Lands, in the jungle play-ground of Pumbaa and Timon.

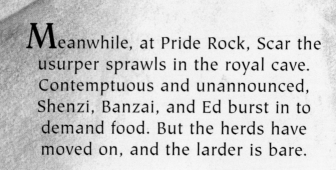

Meanwhile, at Pride Rock, Scar the usurper sprawls in the royal cave. Contemptuous and unannounced, Shenzi, Banzai, and Ed burst in to demand food. But the herds have moved on, and the larder is bare.

One glorious African night,
Simba, Pumbaa, and Timon sprawl in
a jungle clearing, gazing at the stars.

Simba recalls another starry night
and his father's reassuring words.

Overcome by melancholy, Simba goes off by
himself. Flopping to the ground, he loosens
seed floss from a milkweed plant.

A breeze from the cooling plain below lifts the seeds high into the starry sky and carries them toward an ancient tree.

A hand snatches the seed floss from the air. Rafiki sees what he has snared and dives into the tree. In a big tortoise shell, he combines the floss with the contents of a gourd, interprets the signs in the mixture, and laughs. . . .

Simba is alive!

Pumbaa stalks a plump and tasty bug.
Too late he spots a pair of hungry eyes.
The hunter is the hunted.

A lioness springs at the trapped warthog and all seems lost till, with a roar, Simba dashes from the trees.

The lions battle in the
dirt, Simba gaining the
upper hand until,
with a crafty flip, the
lioness pins him.

Simba cannot believe
that Nala has found him!
Nala cannot believe
that Simba is alive!

Simba is still king. This is Nala's
firm belief—a point of view that
Simba does not share.

Together after so many years, Simba and
Nala feel the stirring of secret longings,
the reawakening of childhood dreams.

Simba and Nala wander through the enchanted
landscape. Nala tells Simba how Scar and his
hyena hoodlums have laid waste the Pride
Lands. Still Simba insists he will never return.

Confused by the news Nala has
brought him, Simba seeks solitude
and guidance from the stars.

But the voices of the former kings
are silent, and soon his reverie is
interrupted by a curious song:

"Asante sana.
Squash banana.
We we nugu.
Mi mi apana."

${}^{\text{T}}$elling Simba that his father is alive, Rafiki orders the bewildered lion to follow him.

Simba gazes into the waters of a pool and sees the image of a full-grown lion there, but it is merely his reflection. Disappointment overcomes him once again, but then he hears Mufasa's voice!

The darkness begins to shimmer. Mufasa's spectral image appears, an awesome presence filling the air with supernatural radiance, as if some star has fallen to earth.

"Look inside yourself, Simba. You will find that you are more than what you have become. You must take your place in the Circle of Life. . . .

Remember who you are."

The ghost has vanished. Rafiki reappears and with his stick he teaches a lesson: sometimes the past can hurt, but it will hurt more if you run away than if you face its consequences.

The rightful king goes to claim his throne.

Simba speeds toward Pride Rock, but when he reaches the borders of his kingdom, he finds a scene of utter desolation.

As storm clouds gather, Nala arrives to fight at Simba's side—Timon and Pumbaa, too— and together they move onward to do whatever must be done.

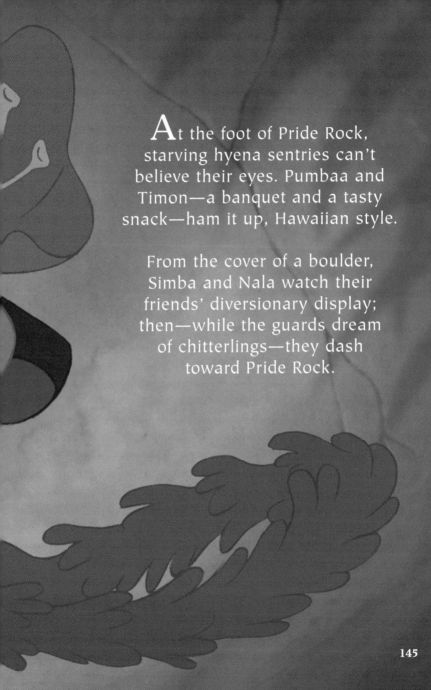

At the foot of Pride Rock, starving hyena sentries can't believe their eyes. Pumbaa and Timon—a banquet and a tasty snack—ham it up, Hawaiian style.

From the cover of a boulder, Simba and Nala watch their friends' diversionary display; then—while the guards dream of chitterlings—they dash toward Pride Rock.

As thunder rumbles all around, Scar calls on Sarabi, Simba's mother, demanding that her hunting parties scour the land for food.

Flashes of lightning set the bushes afire. Flames throw Simba's noble head and muscular body into silhouette.

For a moment, Scar panics, believing Mufasa has returned to haunt him. Simba nuzzles his mother, assuring her that it is he, back to fulfill his destiny. Seeing that Simba, not Mufasa, is his foe, Scar feels his confidence return.

Simba admits his past mistakes, failing to notice that Scar has backed him up against a precipice.

Simba slips and hangs from the rock, seeming completely at Scar's mercy just as Mufasa had been years before. Gloating, Scar recalls Mufasa's death.

Simba pins Scar and forces him to confess to the listening pride that it was he, not Simba, who caused Mufasa's death.

As the Pride Lands burn, Simba and Scar are locked in mortal combat.

The battle is joined once more, with lionesses clawing at hyenas' throats and Rafiki wielding his staff with furious skill.

To save himself, Scar lies again—not realizing that his closest allies are listening as he betrays them.

Giving his uncle one last chance, Simba tells Scar to flee. Scar capitulates. Another trick. Scar lunges at Simba once again, but Simba sends his father's assassin flying off the ledge.

Scar lands in the burning brush, Pride Rock at his back. Led by Shenzi, hyenas advance upon him through the flames. Friends, Scar calls them. But they are friends no more.

Simba reunites with Nala and the pride, and then, through smoke and rain, Rafiki appears once more and motions for the youthful king to take his rightful place.

King at last, Simba climbs through the rain to the summit of Pride Rock.

Simba looks up to the heavens once again and sees the clouds part to reveal an ocean of stars. Distant thunder rumbles, and the new king hears the old king's voice:

"Remember!"

In answer, Simba lets out a mighty roar.

The Pride Lands return to life. Tender shoots
and sweet grasses bring the great herds
back to the water hole, and the union of Simba
and Nala brings a new cub into the world.

The sacred ceremony is repeated. Rafiki
holds the infant aloft for all to see, and the
world resounds with song once more.
The Circle of Life continues.

The art used in this book was created by the artists of Disney Feature Animation, who are listed here:

Kathy Altieri

Ruben Aquino

Kathy Bailey

Doug Ball

Tom Bancroft

James Baxter

Linda Bel

Aaron Blaise

Dave Bossert

Brenda Chapman-Lima

Brian Clift

Charles Colladay

Lorna Cook

Guy Deel

Andreas Deja

Lou Dellarosa

Tony Derosa

Jeff Dickson

Nick Domingo

Gregory Drolette

Mark Empey

Thom Enriquez

Tony Fucile

Andy Gaskill

Mac George

Vance Gerry

Ed Ghertner

Dean Gordon

Joe Haidar

Kevin Harkey

Mark Henn

Jason Herschaft

Ron Husband

Iva Itchevska

Barry Johnson

Broose Johnson

Mike Jones

Christopher Keene

Ted Kierscey

Jorgen Klubien

Nancy Kniep

Alex Kupershmidt

Vera Lanpher-Pacheco

Larry Leker

Burny Mattinson

Gregory Martin

Peter Megow

Mike Merell

Don Moore

David Mooy

Jean Morel

John Ripa

Chris Sanders

Tom Shannon

Richard Sluiter

Bob Smith

Michael Surrey

Dan Tanaka

Alex Topete

Gary Trousdale

Ellen Woodbury

Kelvin Yasuda